RABBI HARVEY vs.
THE WISDOM KID

 A GRAPHIC NOVEL OF
DUELING JEWISH FOLKTALES
IN THE WILD WEST

STEVE SHEINKIN

For People of All Faiths, All Backgrounds

JEWISH LIGHTS Publishing

Woodstock, Vermont
www.jewishlights.com

Rabbi Harvey vs. the Wisdom Kid:
A Graphic Novel of Dueling Jewish Folktales in the Wild West

2010 Quality Paperback Edition, First Printing
@ 2010 by Steve Sheinkin

Library of Congress Cataloging-in-Publication Data
Sheinkin, Steve.
  Rabbi Harvey vs. the wisdom kid : a graphic novel of dueling Jewish folktales in the wild West / Steve Sheinkin.—Quality paperback ed.
     p. cm.
  Includes bibliographical references.
  ISBN-13: 978-1-58023-422-1 (quality pbk.)
  ISBN-10: 1-58023-422-4 (quality pbk.)
  1. Graphic novels. I. Title. II. Title: Rabbi Harvey versus the wisdom kid.
  PN6727.S495R34 2009
  741.5'973—dc22

                                                    2009046014

10 9 8 7 6 5 4 3 2 1
Manufactured in China
Cover design: Jenny Buono
Cover art: Steve Sheinkin

For People of All Faiths, All Backgrounds
Published by Jewish Lights Publishing
A Division of LongHill Partners, Inc.
Sunset Farm Offices, Route 4, P.O. Box 237
Woodstock, VT 05091
Tel: (802) 457-4000   Fax: (802) 457-4004
www.jewishlights.com

CONTENTS

INTRODUCTION

Back in my Hebrew school days I knew a real rabbi named Harvey. I'm not sure he was very wise, though. I remember once asking him why he became a rabbi. "I don't know," he said. "It seemed like something to do."

That sort of sums up my Hebrew school experience—it was something that had to be done. Wasn't I, by learning the essential teachings and traditions of Judaism, being forged into a vital link in the sacred chain of tradition stretching all the way back to Abraham and Moses? Maybe, but I missed that.

In my defense, I did sense that there was *something* interesting in this Judaism stuff. My father was a serious student of Kabbalah (before you could learn it at a weekend seminar) and I used to question him about this mysterious field. Fantastic phrases from his response swirled in my head: "ancient knowledge … healing the world … very powerful … even dangerous." I asked him to teach me a bit. He said I wasn't nearly ready. You had to be at least forty years old, for one thing. You had to be married, for the stability family brings. And you had to be a scholar of Torah and Talmud. I thought, "Oh, forget it, I'll never be any of that." Now, to my astonishment, I'm two of the three. Not the scholar.

But the good news is, my Jewish education is still inching forward, mostly because I get to keep working on these Rabbi Harvey books. As with the first two Harvey adventures, I read thousands of Jewish stories to find just the right ones for this new volume. While the previous books were made up of standalone stories, this new book is one narrative, similar in plot structure to a classic Hollywood western. Unlike most westerns I've seen, however, the story here is made up of bits and pieces of Jewish folktales and teachings, Midrash, Talmudic wisdom, and Hassidic legends. In addition to Harvey's familiar adversaries, I've added a new one: Rabbi "Wisdom Kid" Ruben. Having a villainous rabbi finally allowed me to include several stories I've always loved but have never been able to use—tales that just didn't seem to fit Harvey's style. You'll see what I mean.

Looking ahead several years, I wonder what my own children's Hebrew school experience will be like. I don't know if I'll be much of a mentor, but at least I can share Rabbi Harvey with them. In the hope they'll enjoy Harvey— and, as I continue to do, learn from him—this book is for Anna and David.

HARVEY IN PARADISE

One fine fall day near the town of Elk Spring, Colorado, high in the Rocky Mountains, Solomon Bloom III, a banker from Denver, was struggling to stay afloat in the rushing current of the Black Bear River.

Help!

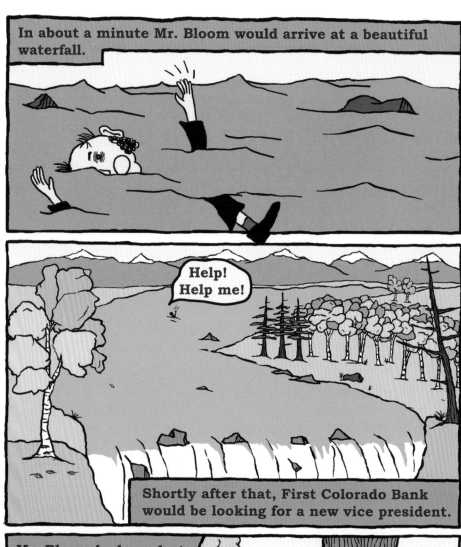

In about a minute Mr. Bloom would arrive at a beautiful waterfall.

Help! Help me!

Shortly after that, First Colorado Bank would be looking for a new vice president.

Mr. Bloom had one last chance. Between the banker and the falls sat Rabbi Harvey, famous throughout the West for his love of learning, justice, and fresh trout.

The Rabbi put a new worm on his hook and cast the line. But his mind did not seem to be on his fishing.

They're just not biting today.

In fact, he was thinking about Abigail, former gold miner and current school teacher in Elk Spring.

And he was thinking about a ring he had ordered from a San Francisco jeweler.

So, Abigail, how would you feel about getting married? No, I can do better.... Let's see.... So, Abby, I was, well, thinking about marriage. To you, I mean, if you're not too busy.... *Uch*, terrible. Come on, Rabbi, think....

Help! Fisherman!

Say, that was good pie. Maybe I could bake some for our wedding, if—

Hold on, I think someone's calling me.

Over here in the water! Help!

Rabbi Harvey sprang into action: he immediately began commenting.

That's a very foolish place to be swimming!

Does it look like I'm swimming, you idiot?

My mistake.

The Rabbi waded into the river.

Grab hold!

Mr. Bloom was saved.

Got it!

Both men collapsed on the riverbank.

The men's clothing dried in the sun as they walked toward town. Mr. Bloom offered to buy the Rabbi dinner. Harvey accepted.

So, you're the famous Rabbi Harvey.

MR. BLOOM: My mother speaks of you often.

RABBI HARVEY: I can't quite get used to the idea of being famous.

MR. BLOOM: She's ... um ... not a fan.

RABBI HARVEY: Oh.

The Rabbi suggested Sara's Cafe, which offered two-for-one pan-fried steak on Tuesday. Luckily, it was Tuesday.

This is not the most tender piece of meat I have ever eaten.

No, tenderness is not their specialty. But how about that mushroom gravy?

It's okay, I guess. But tell me, Rabbi, what can I do to repay you? Surely I owe you more than a lousy piece of fried meat.

Don't worry about it. Saving you was the best exercise I've had in weeks.

I insist, Rabbi. I can't have people saying I don't repay my debts. *Me*, a banker!

I suppose the school could use some new books.

No, no, it has to be something for *you*. Something you've always wanted.

I really can't think of anything. Pass the salt.

Mr. Bloom pressed the Rabbi to name a gift. The Rabbi continued insisting that the meal was plenty.

This appeared to annoy the banker. But actually, things were going exactly according to his plan.

Late that evening two men paid a visit to the Rabbi's office.

In one quick move, they grabbed the sleeping Rabbi, tied his hands, and put him in a large sack.

Hmm ... I can never tell if I'm dreaming or not.

The men walked to a nearby forest.

Heavier than he looks.

They took the Rabbi out of the bag and tied him to a large tree.

I think this is actually happening. How strange.

Then the men left without saying a word.

Several hours passed. The sun came up.

Whoever has done this, please come out and state your business. The town fair begins this morning, and I still have to set up my booth.

Forget about that booth, Rabbi!

Could it be one of my Talmud students? Perhaps that Hillel vs. Shammai exam *was* a little difficult.

But it was not a student.

Hello there, Rabbi! How are you this morning?

Fine.

Glad to hear it, friend. Now, I suppose you're wondering why you're here? Simple. You refused my offer of a gift.

Let me explain. See, you saved my life, and I wanted to give you something special. I asked myself: what's the greatest gift you could give to a rabbi?

That's when I decided: I'll give you the chance to prove you would die for your beliefs. And you did it!

That's gotta score you big points with the Big Sheriff!

Tell the truth, Rabbi. Are you thrilled with my present?

I wouldn't use the word "thrilled."

But we're even now, aren't we?

I mean, we gave each other priceless gifts!

I'm only concerned that your gift was a bit *too* priceless.

Step down to the river with me, and I'll give you one final present.

STUMP THE RABBIS

Harvey took a few sips, then got back to work.

If you're so smart, Rabbi, build me a barn up in the sky.

Sure, you put the lumber in the sky, I'll come build your barn.

Next!

I'm sure one of these boys stole cookies from my booth, Rabbi.

I see. But we must assume each is innocent, unless proven guilty.

Unfortunately, it is clear to me that one of you took the cookies. And it is about to become clear to everyone. *Painfully* clear.

You see, the cookie thief ... I'm afraid his hat is on fire.

Yes, it's beginning to smoke. Oh my, that looks quite uncomfortable.

Get it off!

The cookies were paid for.

The next person in line stepped up.

I'm not sure what to do, Rabbi. There's this beggar fellow who comes to my home at least once a week, asking for food. Don't get me wrong, I give.

But when I invite him in to join my family in a few prayers, he won't do it. I try to get him to at least say a blessing over the bread I give him, but he refuses.

From now on: no blessing, no bread.

yawn ... I think that would be a great mistake.

How so, Rabbi?

Rabbi Harvey opened his mouth to answer. Or perhaps to yawn again. In either case, before he could speak—

Sometimes it is best to act as if there were no God.

The Rabbi turned to see who had spoken. He was surprised to see a new booth next to his.

STUMP THE RABBI 5¢

STUMP THE RABBI 1¢

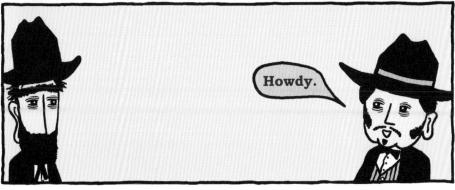

Howdy.

Umm ... why would I want to act as if there were no God?

Step over here, sir, and I will gladly tell you. For just one penny.

Excuse me a moment.

Certainly.

When this poor man comes to you in need, tell yourself there is no God. **But why?**

Because then you will act as if there is no one in the world to help—no one except yourself.

Fine, but ... he has to say his prayers, right? I mean, feeding the body is one thing, but what about his soul?

Ah, but you see, sir, you are responsible for *his* body, and *your* soul.

People seemed reluctant to lose their place in line.

The next two men stepped up to Rabbi Harvey's table.

So I get on the stagecoach in Leadville, headed for Elk Spring. This gentleman is sitting in the stagecoach already.

I politely ask him what time it is. And he says: "Drop dead, pal!"

He should apologize, right?

I was justified.

Rabbi Ruben interrupted:

Sir, I don't see how you can—

He was justified.

The men walked over to Rabbi Ruben's table.

You got on the stagecoach and asked this man the time?

That's right.

You were going to be sitting on the stagecoach for hours. Did knowing the exact time really matter?

The crowd cheered the new rabbi. Some people began leaving Rabbi Harvey's line and lining up before Rabbi Ruben.

That was pretty good, actually.

Does our esteemed rabbi have something to add?

As the Talmud says, when a fool is silent, he too is counted among the wise.

That sparked a duel of Talmudic teachings.

Two ears, one mouth: hear much, say little.

Silence is good for the wise. How much more so for the foolish.

The actions of a fool must not serve as a precedent.

When the wise is angry, he is no longer wise.

Who is strong? He who masters his evil impulses.

God created the Evil Impulse—and the Torah as its antidote.

One does not drink poison because one knows the antidote.

If one person tells you you're a donkey, ignore him. If two tell you, buy yourself a saddle.

Sorry, you lost me there.

Let's get back to business, shall we?

Some rabbis have long lines of customers waiting.

Others, not so much.

The next customer:

So God really exists, Rabbi?

Certainly.

Prove it. Show God to me.

You see that giant yellow ball up in the sky? Take a close look at it.

The girl did as she was told.

Yowch! My eyes!

You can't even look at the sun, which is just one of God's many servants. So, you silly child, how do you expect to see God?

Next!

So young, and yet, so wise.

These questions are simply too easy for you, my son. Perhaps Rabbi Harvey would care to pose a challenge of his own?

Perhaps not, Ma.

Rabbi Harvey was fast asleep.

ZZZZZ

So he did not see Mr. Bloom, the banker, stop by Rabbi Ruben's booth.

Well, Ma, looks like our delightfully fiendish little plan is off to a good start.

Yes, thanks to your fine work, *tateleh*.

It was nothing. Just a pleasant little swim.

Not that I needed your help to outwit Rabbi Harvey.

Oh, admit it, I softened him up for you, little brother.

I'm called Rabbi Ruben now.

To me you're still just a kid.

Kid Wisdom, to be precise.

Such wonderful boys....

FOUR BROTHERS, TWO RABBIS

By the next morning, everyone in town was talking about the new rabbi.

You should have seen this fella, Mort. Such incredibly quick thinking!

In the dining room of *Bubbe's* Inn.

How about the learning! The years of study!

And I hear his wisdom was nothing to sneeze at.

I sort of enjoyed his humor.

And you say nothing about his modesty?

So now, it seemed, there were two rabbis in Elk Spring.

Morning, Ma.

Here's the original:

Maybe tonight will be the night? I'll invite her over for dinner, roast a chicken—

A farmer named Nathan interrupted Harvey's thoughts.

Morning, Rabbi. You're looking much better today.

Thanks, Nathan, feeling better. What can I do for you?

You know my brother Ari and I share a big farm, right Rabbi? We split our harvest fifty-fifty. And this year's beet crop has been huge.

But the thing is, I've got my wife, Ruth, to run my half of the farm with me.

And we've got five kids now. They'll take over as we get older. But my brother, he lives over in his house all alone.

So I figured he could use a few extra beets to sell. You know, set the money aside for a rainy day. Though, of course, he'd be too proud to accept anything from me.

So late last night, right about midnight, I filled a small wagon with beets and pulled it over to his place.

I dumped the beets in the bins in his barn. Then I went home and went to sleep.

yawn

Now here's the crazy part: this morning, when I went out to my own barn, the bins were still full of beets.

?

Just as if I'd never taken any of them out.

I'm sure I didn't dream the whole thing, Rabbi. You think it was some sort of miracle? You know, like the Hanukkah oil, except with root vegetables?

And everything just seems to go wrong for him—jobs, women, dental work, you name it. It's really got him down. I'd give him money, I've got plenty, but he won't take it, he's too proud.

Try giving him money in secret. Perhaps fill a bag and leave it near his shack? He'll think he stumbled upon it.

And he'll believe his luck has finally turned! I'll do it tonight! Do you know you're a genius, Rabbi?

The thought has crossed my mind.

Sam left the inn.

Just outside he ran into—

Oh, uh, hi there, Rabbi.

Morning, Sam.

They make a nice fried egg.

I'll have to try it.

The men wished each other a good day. Then Harvey walked toward the home of Ari, the brother of Nathan, the man who had come to see him that morning.

But it was the weirdest thing.... When it got light this morning I looked in my own barn, and the beet bins were just as full as they'd been the night before!

Amazing.

What do you figure happened?

Hard to say. Why not try again tonight? I'll watch from a nearby hill and attempt to determine the cause of this strange event.

But do me one favor. Bring the load of beets to your brother a bit earlier. Maybe about midnight?

I don't know if I could sit up there all night. Been a bit short on sleep lately.

No problem, Rabbi.

Rabbi Harvey headed back to town. Meanwhile, Rabbi Ruben was on his way out of town.

Maybe I can duck behind that pine tree—no, too late.

Howdy!

That is a great sin, to think like that. Why, think of all there is to be grateful for!

Like what?

Do this for me, Eli. Tomorrow morning, before leaving your home, tie a handkerchief tightly over your eyes. Walk all the way to town blind-folded.

As you struggle in darkness, you will begin to recognize how blessed you truly are! You will begin to appreciate that beauty surrounds you every day—if only you would take the trouble to see it!

I'll try it, Rabbi!

Rabbi Ruben walked back toward town.

Did you ever hear tell of sweet Betsy from Pike, Who crossed the wide prairie with her lover, Ike?

That night, a little before midnight, Rabbi Harvey found a somewhat comfortable place on a hill overlooking Nathan and Ari's farm.

I think I see Nathan coming.

Excellent, here comes Ari as well.

The next morning, Rabbi Ruben returned to Eli's cabin.

But this time the Rabbi did not knock on the door.

Very soon, the door opened.

Okay, here we go. Hey, this really is pretty hard.

Whoa, careful of the rock!

I never even noticed a rock in front of my house. And it's probably beautiful!

That rabbi was so right! I've lived without ever really seeing! Ow!

DUEL ON MAIN STREET

42

Goodness, no. Far more precious.

The men seemed interested.

Let's have a look-see.

I'm afraid I'm quite busy with my studies, gentlemen.

The men were determined to know what I had on the ship.

They looked through all the ship's cargo.

They searched on deck.

Their thoroughness was quite praiseworthy.

Annoyed at not finding my goods, the merchants didn't notice the storm brewing in the East.

Before I had time to dress, the rain and wind and waves clobbered our poor vessel. We were taking on water and beginning to sink.

There was only one chance—we had to lighten the ship by throwing all our cargo overboard. This alone saved us from certain death, allowing the ship to reach the nearest port.

I never did recover my clothing.

The merchants were not much better off.

I walked into town. The merchants followed.

There I began to teach. A little Torah, a little Talmud, a little of my own material.

And so then I said to Rabbi Simeon....

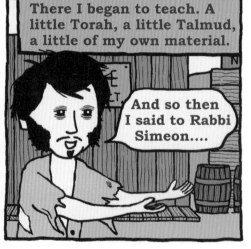

Thank you, friends! Thank you! I'm glad to share more of my tales with you!

More than glad! Of course, you wouldn't expect a carpenter to work without payment. Or a shoemaker. Is wisdom less valuable than cabinets? Than footwear?

I feel like I haven't eaten in days.

But I should really go out there, shouldn't I?

I'm counting on all of you to contribute your fair share to the Wisdom Barrel. We don't want a repeat of something that once happened back East, a memory that still pains me greatly.

You see, I was planning a huge banquet to celebrate the wedding of an honored teacher. I asked my fellow students to each contribute a bottle of wine.

The plan was to pour the bottles into a large barrel, then pull the barrel to the wedding party.

What I could never have imagined:

We're all pouring our bottles into one huge barrel. Why waste good wine? I'm going to pour in water, and no one will ever know the difference.

Everyone had the exact same idea.

No one will know.

BOOTS

And when it came time to serve our beloved master and his beautiful bride ...

... all that came from the barrel was water.

I was on a boat, crossing San Francisco Bay. For reasons that are not entirely clear, the oars fell into the sea.

Oh, not again!

Again?

We drifted helplessly. We soon became very hungry. My fellow passenger was a wealthy matzo merchant traveling with a large crate of product.

But he refused to open the crate.

Passover's coming, son. You know what I can get for this stuff on shore?

Please, sir, allow us to purchase just one piece.

A burnt one would be fine.

Listen, pal, I'm only looking out for my own interests.

Your little story reminds me of a very great thing I once said.

Somehow I am not surprised.

I had just begun teaching back East, and a student, a gifted young scholar, came to me, greatly distressed.

Tell me, Rabbi, please. How can I drive off the evil, the suffering ... the darkness that surrounds all of us?

Take this broom to the cellar beneath the school. Sweep out the darkness from the room.

The student swept for hours. But the room remained dark.

Take this stick to the cellar. Beat the darkness until it leaves the room.

But the room remained dark.

Take this candle to the cellar and light it.

Finally, the darkness retreated.

Hey, it's working!

Let each of us be a candle. Let each of us light a small patch of darkness.

I didn't know we were supposed to bring props.

We've been over this, friends. Cheers are nice, but why not let your coins do the cheering! Let them rattle and ring in the Wisdom Barrel!

WISDOM

Perhaps you'd like to make a small offering, Rabbi H?

There's the one about the three brothers and the ring ... or maybe the one with the fish that swallowed the jewel ...

Sorry, what?

Now, I used to think about this tradition quite a lot. And I used to wonder: who will be my neighbor for all eternity? One day I had a dream.

The identity of my neighbor appeared to me in glittering letters of gold.

Amos, the gold miner from Red Mountain?

I confess I was disappointed, even offended. I'm no Maimonides, granted, but I've done a bit of learning.

This Amos doesn't sound like much of a scholar.

What are we supposed to talk about for the next million years?

So I set out for the town of Red Mountain to find this fellow.

My journey took me to a remote mining camp, more than two miles high in the mountains.

I stopped at the general store and asked around for a miner named Amos.

He don't ever come into town.

Not even since we put up the temple tent.

I got directions to Amos's mining shack.

Clearly I am far less worthy than I fooled myself into believing.

I finally found the place.

Howdy! Anyone home?

What do you want?

I'm Rabbi Harvey of Elk Spring.

That's not what I asked.

I asked to come inside. Amos shrugged and returned to his dinner.

This looks pretty bad for you, Harvey. But let's not judge too hastily ... let's learn a bit more about this man.

Am I being punished for the time I accidentally ate French toast on Passover?

But you give a bit to charity, I imagine?

Give what, my toenail clippings?

Hello! Anyone home?

Now what?

A man in a suit stepped inside.

There is gold on this property, but you will never find it.

I know, I know, I'm saying the wrong prayers.

Perhaps. But more to the point, the gold is locked in hard rocks deep underground, requiring heavy machines, capital investment. The Samson Mining Corporation has authorized me to offer you two hundred and fifty dollars for your claim.

Two-fifty? I'll go get the claim certificate right now!

The miner leapt up and ran into the next room.

Friend of yours?

Neighbor.

The miner returned moments later.

Sorry, I can't give you the certificate.

Very well, sir. I am prepared to offer you three hundred dollars.

I could order that crate of chopped liver I've been eying!

Still, I can't give it to you.

I can go as high as five hundred.

Sorry, I can't.

Fine, then. Seven-fifty.

Wish I could.

One thousand.

cough! cough!

Where'd I put my pants?

Okay, I'll go get the certificate.

Charming neighbor.

Not my first choice.

Moments later.

Alright, pal, here it is.

And here is your thousand dollars.

I didn't even enjoy the French toast.

I can't take a thousand dollars.

We had a deal!

We did, that's true.

So take your money and give me the paper.

Not so fast.

I keep the certificate under the mattress, see? But when I went to get it, I saw my father was sleeping on the bed. He doesn't sleep so good these days, and I would never disturb his rest for any amount of money. That's why I came back without the paper.

But then I heard him coughing and talking. I knew he must have woken up. So I went to get the paper.

Anyways, a deal's a deal. I said I'd sell for two-fifty, so that's what you owe me.

How'd you sleep, Papa? How about some beans?

cough, cough.

Sir, I would be honored to be your neighbor in the World to Come.

You try talking to this rabbi fellow, Papa. I have no idea what he's saying.

WICK HARDW & TOO

Just then a rider raced into town.

Rabbi Harvey! Letter for Rabbi Harvey!

Where do I know you from?

Umm ... Friday night services?

!

Rabbi Harvey read the letter.

Then, without saying a word, he ran to the stable, jumped on his horse, and raced out of town.

WOLFIE THE WISE

Rabbi Harvey was still about ten miles from his destination: the town of Helms Falls.

Which gives us time to check in on some very important news from that little town.

Just a few days before, two strangers had arrived in town.

WASSERMAN & SON BARBERS

TOWN HELM

It was Big Milt Wasserman and his son, Wolfie.

Once the most feared father-and-son outlaw team east of Nevada.

Once and future, pal.

See, about a year ago, they'd been disarmed by Rabbi Harvey.

I've asked you multiple times to stop mentioning that.

Sorry, Big Milt.

Now Milt was out for revenge. As the wagon approached town, he described the plan.

Helms Falls is looking for a sheriff, and I'll get the job, see? And once we get hold of the town, we move on to step two—are you listening, son?

Sorry, Pops, I was thinking.

What about?

Not sure.

Why not, pray tell?

I'm not done yet.

It's no wonder I can't get ahead ...

A few minutes later, on a hill above Helms Falls.

Push! Harder!

Milt got out of the wagon and took a closer look.

Then he noticed a pile of coats on the ground.

Hey, free coats!

Push! Push!

WASSERMAN & SON BARBERS

Milt and Wolfie took the coats to their wagon. Then they walked back toward the strange scene at the mill.

Remember, I do all the talking.

Okay, let's take a break!

Howdy, friends. Might I inquire what in the name of Solomon's ring you are doing?

We built this mill up here.

Only it doesn't work.

Of course not, it's a watermill! Water is required to turn the wheel. You should have built it next to the river.

But it looks much nicer up here.

Besides, water isn't the problem.

We tried pouring buckets of water on the wheel. Nothing happened.

Anyway, it's clearly not working up here, so we figured we might as well push it closer to town.

Look! We've really made progress!

We put our coats down by the mill this morning, and we've pushed the mill so far, we can't even see the coats anymore!

A town of fools. Makes my job even easier.

That's enough for today, folks! Let's head back to town!

I have an idea. Why don't we roll the waterwheel down the hill right now?

Brilliant! One less thing to move tomorrow.

But hold on. What if the wheel rolls so far that we can't find it?

This really got the people to thinking.

A fine question, my friends. You are familiar, of course, with the fact that the earth spins on its axis, about twenty-three degrees from the vertical.

Alright, imagine my left hand is the earth, and the sun is—

People light stoves in winter!

I told you, *I* do the talking.

But Pops, listen.

People light stoves in winter, which causes the air to heat up. So by summer time, it's hot outside.

Since it's hot, people don't use their stoves, maybe just a little for cooking. The air cools down, and by the time winter arrives, it's cold out again!

The panel seemed to approve.

Here's another puzzle. Which is more important, the sun or the moon?

Well, that may be subjective, but you realize, of course, that the so-called light of the moon is merely a reflection of—

The moon is more important!

We suspected as much. But why?

Simple. The sun shines during the day, when it's already light. So who needs it?

But the moon is more important, because it gives light at night—when otherwise it would be completely dark!

Wonderful! We have one last question, a real riddle.

Fire away, friends.

It is well known that when you drop a piece of buttered bread, it falls with the buttered side down. But the other day I dropped a piece, and it landed with the buttered side up. What happened?

Simple. You buttered your bread on the wrong side.

Congratulations.

You've got the job.

A development which is about to become very important to our story.

RABBI HARVEY FOR THE DEFENSE

Speaking of our story, Rabbi Harvey has just arrived in the town of Helms Falls.

Thanks, Abe.

Wolfie had been sheriff for only three days, but he and his deputy, Big Milt, had been busy.

Very busy.

Can you tell me where the town jail is located?

In the back of the saloon.

Harvey hurried to the saloon.

I understand a prisoner is being held in here?

Back in the storeroom, with the deputy. Suppose we should have a proper prison, though we never really needed one.

We only once ever had a serious crime. Had to hang the baker.

Hang him! Why? What had he done?

Nothing. But the blacksmith committed murder.

So why not punish the blacksmith?

He's the only one in town.

We had two bakers.

Take me to the prisoner right away.

In the room in the back of the saloon.

I got the note. What's happening here, Abby?

Well, well, how entertaining. We were just talking about you.

Big Milt Wasserman.

Little Rabbi Harvey.

Heard you became a barber.

I'm a lawman now, like you.

Which means you have to actually obey the law.

I always obey the law— Big Milt's law.

I'm not familiar with that particular statute.

Allow me to enlighten you.

You guys done yet?

Yes, sorry. Why exactly are you holding this woman?

She robbed the town bank several years ago. Probably thought she'd gotten away with it. But yesterday I sent some men to arrest her and bring her here to face the consequences.

Now, now, ma'am. Several reliable witnesses have identified you as the bandit. And this town is committed to swift, firm-handed justice.

What an incredible load of—

You can't really mean to hang her!

You guessed it, *Rebbe*.

And the best part: you're just in time to see the show.

Ten minutes later.

Well, friends. Shall we get this sad business over with?

Just a minute, Milt! Since Abigail is about to die, let her give us her magical bandana!

Magical bandana?

Magical bandana?

Yes, the one with special powers!

Abigail played along, though she had no idea what the Rabbi was talking about.

Oh, you mean this one? That I got from that strange old peddler?

Right! You don't need its powers anymore, so why not let us have it?

Hey, isn't that Rabbi Harvey?

My friends, this is no ordinary piece of cloth! Lay it flat on the ground, wait five seconds, then lift it—underneath you will find a nugget of pure gold!

But it will not work for just anyone. The person setting down the bandana must never have taken anything that did not belong to him. Or her.

Oh, now I see where he's going with this.

You're right, Rabbi, I might as well give it away. It's no use to me now.

Of course, I am unable to demonstrate my bandana's magical powers, on account of the whole bank robbery thing. Perhaps Rabbi Harvey will show us!

Abigail managed to untie her bandana. She handed it down to the Rabbi.

Shall I demonstrate this fantastic fabric?

Yes!

Let's see that gold, Rabbi!

Certainly! Gather round, ladies and gentlemen!

But wait a bit ...

I just remembered. Once, when I was a young boy, I snuck several coins from my father's drawer. The magic bandana will not work for me!

Anyone want a priceless treasure?

Right here!

The man stepped forward and took the bandana from the Rabbi's hand.

He laid it flat on the street.

He waited five seconds, then lifted it.

Nothing.

Fine, I admit that I sometimes take watermelons from my neighbor's garden.

I had no idea the bandana was that strict.

Anyone else?

I'll pass.

"To get Harvey here?"

"That's right. All part of *Bubbe's* master plan."

"We've been working out the details for months."

"She and her son get the town of Elk Spring. And I get Rabbi Harvey."

"Ah, Bad *Bubbe* Bloom.... Looks, brains, her own business ..."

"But I must stay focused on my work."

Milt turned to address the crowd.

"The Rabbi is correct, we have no right to condemn this poor woman! Sheriff Wolfie and I have agreed to set her free!"

"We do have one more piece of business, however. This morning I was informed by my friends in Elk Spring that money is missing from the town treasury."

"They sent over a handbill describing the prime suspect. Oh yes, here it is."

WANTED

FOR ROBBERY, EMBEZZLEMENT, GIVING UNWANTED ADVICE

RABBI HARVEY

REWARD OF $500

Believed to be unarmed, but still dangerous: avoid matching wits with this man.

ADVICE, WISDOM, MIRACLES

The following morning in Elk Spring.

BUBBE'S INN

RABBI

Should I be a rabbi? ♫
I don't know how to pray.
Should I be a sculptor?
I hate the smell of clay ...

Should I be a shochet?
I cannot use a chalef*. ♫
should I be a teacher?
I don't know an alef....

*shochet: kosher butcher
chalef: butcher's knife

While waiting for breakfast, Rabbi Ruben read a letter from Big Milt. The news from Helms Falls was good.

Excellent work, Milt. Brilliant.

We won't be hearing from Rabbi Harvey any time soon. Looks like this town really needs me now, huh?

Just the opportunity for my young genius.

Oh, you're the true genius of the family, Ma.

These potatoes look a little burnt.

83

The whole family really needs new outfits: husband, children, grand-parents....

Shall we say another hundred and fifty?

At least.

Then there's all the food for the wedding celebration.

I'll need another hundred for that.

Don't forget the wine.

Seventy-five dollars.

At a minimum.

Of course, we'll have to hire musicians. Another fifty. And thirty for the baker, for the special cake.

Got it.

Rabbi Ruben turned to Hal.

Would you care to assist this woman?

Me? I've got nothing, Rabbi! Zero, with a hole in the middle.

The landowner is dead. Next in line, please!

That's fast work, Rabbi!

Fastest wisdom in the West.

A student stepped forward.

I hope to become a rabbi someday myself, Rabbi.

Any advice?

Tough business, son.

Profitable, though.

Go ahead and test this young man's rabbi potential.

Okay, sure. How?

Never mind, I'll do it.

The student dropped his payment into the barrel. The test began.

Two horse thieves crawl under a fence and into a corral. Each hops on a horse and they ride off.

Back in their dark cave they light a lantern. The light reveals that one thief's face is smudged with mud.

The other's face is clean. Now: which one goes to wash?

I figure it makes sense that the dirty one would wash—

Wrong!

A fine rabbi you'd make! Listen, the thieves light the lantern and look at each other, right?

The one with the dirty face sees that his partner's face is clean, so he assumes his is clean as well. But the one with the clean face sees the mud on his partner's face, so he figures his is dirty too, and goes to wash!

I guess maybe I'm not rabbi material.

Better to find out now. Glad I could help, son.

Yeah, thanks.

Meanwhile, the young farmhand was having some serious second thoughts.

I can't believe the old guy's really dead! Just like that! One second, living and breathing, and the next....

Sure he could be cruel and stingy, but to have him killed! Who am I to decide who lives and who dies?

Rabbi Harvey says that taking a life is like destroying an entire world. So, great, now I've destroyed a world!

Also, I could go to jail.

The man turned around and raced back toward town.

Wait! Wait, Rabbi! I've made a terrible mistake!

STABLE &

Exactly as expected. Oh, Rabbi, your genius astonishes even me!

Wait, Rabbi!

Back so soon?

I had, *pant, pant,* no right to take that man's life! You have to help me!

What, now you want me to bring your boss back to life? As if this were the world's simplest task?

Well, if there's nothing else, I'll get back to that tricky Talmudic passage on my desk.

WISDOM BARREL

Hey, wait a minute ...

What about me, Rabbi! I paid you twenty dollars!

You're cured, you idiot!

I am?

You were suffering from the sin of pride, correct?

As we have just seen, you have no money, no powers, and no knowledge. So—what do you have to be proud of?

And with that, Rabbi Ruben turned and walked toward the inn.

He shut the door behind him.

BOBBES IN

ABBI.

THE PRETTY GREAT ESCAPE

Inside, Sheriff Wolfie and the bartender were guarding the prisoner.

What's the problem, Rabbi?

Stomachache. Terrible, stabbing pains. Ohhhh, I can't bear it!

Guess he didn't like the prison food.

The bread *was* a bit blue.

I thought that was the butter.

I don't blame you, gentlemen, there's nothing to be done. I just have to suffer through it. Unless....

Unless what?

My aunt Alice used to have this trick to cure stomachaches. Crazy, but it worked.

What was it?

Oh, we couldn't possibly do it.

Why not?

Well for one thing, we don't have enough rope.

Oh, there is a long coil of rope in the corner? Yes, that should be plenty. Now tie me up as tightly as you can, arms and legs, everything.

Harvey is clearly up to something in there.

Abigail listened a moment longer, then walked through town.

He'll bust out, alright. And when he does, he'll need two things: One, his horse, to escape from town.

And two, something decent to eat. He gets cranky on an empty stomach.

Abigail entered the nearest inn.

Good evening, ma'am. I was hoping to get a bite to eat.

Aren't you the one ... from the bank robbery?

They think I won't, but I'll do it!

Exactly as my father used to!

What he could do I can do just as well!

Just a moment.

The inn-keeper left the dining room.

She returned moments later with plates piled high with food.

I forgot we had these last little morsels.

Abigail ate some, and wrapped up the rest for the Rabbi.

Everything to your liking, dear?

Delicious, thank you.

Good, good. Now, I can't help wondering....

You said something about doing what your father used to do?

That's right. He was sometimes refused food.

And if I may ask ... what exactly did he do?

He went to bed hungry.

Meanwhile, in the prison.

Oh, the relief! I'm floating on clouds, gentlemen!

You can untie me now.

Harvey was returned to the crate.

Good old Aunt Alice! Works every time. Now, if only I could get a piece of the saloon's famous gefilte fish, I'd be all set.

Wouldn't mind a nibble, myself.

Got a long night ahead of us.

We're in luck, then. We sit in a storeroom, surrounded by jelly-covered balls of fish!

Indeed, this did appear to be the case.

That all belongs to Gefilte Gil, the saloon owner.

True, true. We mustn't take what isn't ours ...

But wait!

Here's a half-dollar! Serve me up a big piece! And hold on to the coin for the Gefilte Gil.

The bartender took the coin. He served Harvey a plate with gefilte fish and a dollop of fresh horseradish.

It doesn't come with a bit of matzo?

Don't push your luck, Rabbi.

The Rabbi began eating.

Excellent fish. A delicate balance of whitefish and yellow pike, with just enough onion to add roundness and depth.

And the texture ... light, almost airy, firm but not dense.

Perfectly seasoned, I might add.

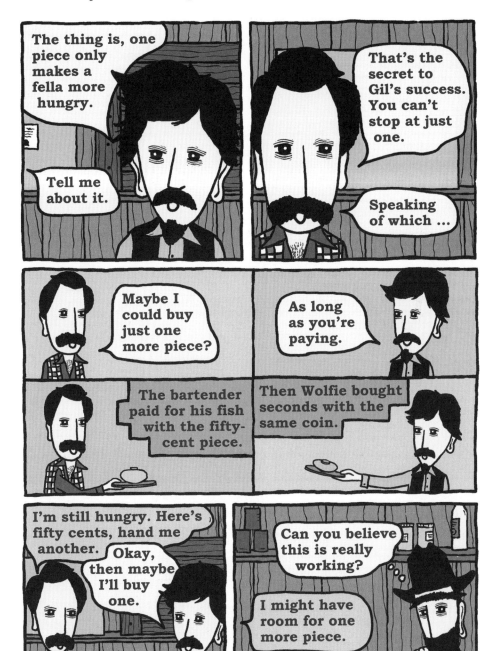

At that very moment, Abigail stood in the street, her pockets bulging with bread.

Now for step two of my plan.

Harvey's horse stood in the stable.

It looked like they meant to keep him there.

For quite some time.

Abigail snuck behind the stable and found a way into the building.

Shhh. Easy, Abe, it's just me.

Outside the stable.

Big Milt should be here any minute to take over. I'll just take one more—

Who the...? What the...?

Morning. Looks like another hot one.

It does, but ... what happened to the horse?

SHOWDOWN AT ELK SPRING

About an hour after Rabbi Harvey's escape, a small crowd gathered outside of *Bubbe's* Inn in Elk Spring. Unlike the day before, the people did not come in search of advice.

The door of the inn soon opened.

Everyone turned to see who had spoken.

Then they turned to see the mule.

Now what did I do?

The mule sleeps on the ground, eats weeds, can even stand silently while being whipped.

It seems our guest is qualified to be a mule.

Though perhaps not a rabbi.

I'll be right down.

So you neither cured the bird nor killed it. According to your own agreement with this woman, you have no right to a payment.

That's our rabbi!

We missed you, Harvey!

Rabbi Ruben gave back the woman's cash.

I do a lovely bird funeral. Reasonable rates.

Rabbi Ruben returning money? *Now* we've witnessed a miracle.

Don't celebrate yet, darling.

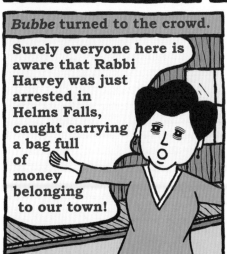

Bubbe turned to the crowd.

Surely everyone here is aware that Rabbi Harvey was just arrested in Helms Falls, caught carrying a bag full of money belonging to our town!

That's right! And it was probably just a fraction of what he has stolen over the years. Is this the kind of man we want as our rabbi?

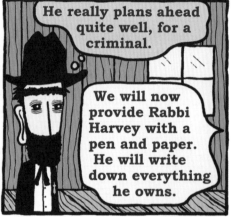

Rabbi Harvey wrote for about ten minutes.

He's sure to leave out something, which will plant a seed of doubt about his honesty.

Pretty small seed.

From such seeds sprout mighty oaks.

Harvey handed his list to Rabbi Ruben.

Okay, I'm done.

What is this? Outrageous lies! You haven't listed your books, your horse! Or your fishing rods or your famous hat! Not even your office!

Actually, the office belongs to the town. At any rate, I only listed my *true* possessions—that is, the things I have given away.

Things I own can be taken from me at any moment, as I have seen all too clearly these last few days.

But the money and items I've given to others—these are my *true* possessions. Only these can never be taken from me.

Now that's what I call a rabbi.

Still the fastest in the West.

What was that crashing sound?

I heard nothing.

I think it was your oak tree falling.

Watch and learn, my child.

After this strange set of signals, Rabbi Ruben turned to the crowd.

Rabbi Harvey is clever with words, let's grant him that. Words are okay, I guess, but I'd rather get back to doing what I love to do—miracles!

I can see!

Oh, the beauty of creation!

The people weren't sure what to think.

?

Now, neighbors, perhaps you'll allow me to go inside and eat my pancakes?

Did you say ... pancakes?

grrgggle

Fresh sliced peaches on top.

And maple syrup?

All the way from Vermont.

It appeared as if the Rabbi might collapse.

But he rallied.

Just a second!

Well, I better not miss the stagecoach, I mean ... what do they look like, anyway?

Nice try, *Bubbe.*

I'm not your *bubbe.*

This stranger has deceived us! But come on, folks, you can hardly doubt the wisdom and wonders you have witnessed in these last few days!

I'll give you a wonder. Last night I had Rabbi Ruben over for dinner, and now I'm wondering where my golden Kiddush cup is!

This is really going too far, people.

All I know is it was there before dinner. Now it's gone.

Seems unlikely that the Rabbi would have stolen your golden cup. Were there any other guests at dinner?

Yes, Harvey, two others.

The three guests from the dinner party stood together.

Did one of you take this cup?

No.

No.

Not me.

These men are probably all telling the truth, but this is a perfect opportunity for me to try out a new device I've been working on.

Not quite a miracle, this invention, but fairly clever, I think.

Harvey asked Abigail to walk with him to his office. Moments later, sounds of sawing and hammering could be heard.

Harvey and Abigail soon emerged carrying a large wooden box.

ELK SPRIN STABLE &

I had no idea you'd been working on a new invention, Harv.

It came as a surprise to me, too.

They set the box down in front of *Bubbe's* Inn.

INN

This is fine, thanks.

Now, inside this box I have placed my little invention. If it is agreeable to you, gentlemen, you will step up to the box one at a time.

Each man will put his arm into the box and feel around for my hat. You can't miss it. When you touch the hat, well ...

Anyone who is telling the truth will feel nothing. But anyone who is lying will get a terrific jolt, quite painful, I'm afraid.

I haven't fine-tuned that part of the invention just yet.

In any case, we'll know right away if one of you has lied to us about the missing cup. Do you agree, gentlemen?

The men agreed.

The first man put his hand into the box. No cry of pain was heard.

The second man did the same. No cry of pain.

Rabbi Ruben took his turn.

No cry of pain.

That's disappointing.

Well, Rabbi Harvey? Looks like you owe Rabbi Ruben an apology.

It does appear that way, doesn't it?

And yet I'm sure the machine is working ...

Let me check one last thing. If I can just ask each of you men to show me the hand you put in the box?

The first man stepped forward. His palm was black with dust.

As I suspected.

The second man's hand was also filthy.

Thank you, sir.

Let me explain. You see, back in my office I rubbed a bit of coal dust onto my hat. That way I could check each man's hand. I would know if he had really touched the hat.

That afternoon, Rabbi Ruben boarded the stagecoach and headed out of town.

See you later, Rabbi!

Harvey sincerely hoped that this would not be the case.

He took the rest of the day off.

He did a little fishing, a little thinking.

Abigail joined him later that afternoon.

STORY SOURCES

As in the first two books in this series, *Rabbi Harvey vs. the Wisdom Kid: A Graphic Novel of Dueling Jewish Folktales in the Wild West* draws upon thousands of years of Jewish teaching and storytelling. My search for material took me to many libraries, and I want to offer special thanks to Lisa Silverman and Joel Tuchman at the Sinai Temple's Blumenthal Library in Los Angeles, and Lynn Feinman at the 92nd Street Y in New York City. For help with Bad *Bubbe's* Yiddish, thanks to the generous folks at the National Yiddish Book Center in Amherst, Massachusetts. Of course, I'm always on the lookout for new material, and I'd be happy to hear any suggestions. Please feel free to e-mail me at steve@rabbiharvey.com.

Harvey in Paradise

This story is based on a strange and darkly funny folktale about a man trying to repay a rabbi for saving his life. I sketched a Rabbi Harvey version of this tale about ten years ago, but kept setting it aside, waiting for the right place to use it. There's not much learned in this tale, but I liked it here because it allowed me to build the mood, and set up the plot twists ahead.

Stump the Rabbis

As usual in these "Stump" stories, the wisdom flies fast and furious. The insight about changing oneself before trying to change the world comes from a Hassidic tale, as does the "sometimes you have to act as if there were no God" teaching. The four-way Talmudic duel allowed me to get in several lines from my notebooks, Talmudic tidbits I've been trying to use for years. Rabbi Ruben's "looking at the sun" trick comes from a tale set in the third century in which the emperor of Rome challenges Rabbi Joshua to prove the existence of "your people's God."

Four Brothers, Two Rabbis

The story of the rich merchant leaving money in a sack for his hard-luck brother is adapted from a traditional tale from Tunisia. The original has the bit about the poor brother blindfolding himself, but, of course, not the part where the evil rabbi swoops in to steal the cash. The story of Nathan and Ari, brother farmers, is based on one of my all-time favorite Jewish tales. In the traditional version, the spot on the road where they meet, each hauling a load of wheat for the other, is the location in Jerusalem where the Temple was eventually built.

Duel on Main Street

This story gave me another chance to throw in many of the gems I've collected over the years. Midrash provides the original version of Ruben's "most valuable merchandise" teaching. His wine story comes from the Hassidic master Rabbi Jacob Krantz of Dubno, who tells this story to a rich man who won't give to charity because he assumes others will. Harvey's "hole in the boat" story comes from a Talmudic teaching by Rabbi Shimon Bar Yochai. I've seen many versions of the tale upon which Harvey's story about his neighbor in the World to Come is based—sometimes the curious rabbi is Rashi, sometimes the Baal Shem Tov. The common theme is that the rabbi's neighbor turns out to be a humble man who does good in his own quiet way.

Wolfie the Wise

I'm often asked why I haven't called upon the brilliant material found in the tales of *The Wise Men of Chelm*. My answer: I couldn't figure out how—until now. The Wolfie character, and the discovery of the town of Helms Falls, gave me the perfect chance to adapt some of Chelm's priceless wisdom.

Rabbi Harvey for the Defense

Rabbi Harvey applies a classic trick in this one, the kind of thing I'm always on the lookout for when reading Jewish tales. In one traditional version of this tale, the condemned man claims to have magic pomegranate seeds, which will sprout instantly into trees—but only for those who have never stolen anything. The king and his advisors are tempted, but pass. Who wouldn't?

Advice, Wisdom, Miracles

Here I got to have fun by allowing a rabbi to grossly misuse Jewish wisdom. The story of the farm hand who wants his boss killed comes from a tale about a Jewish innkeeper in Poland who is cheated and abused by his landlord. In the original, the rabbi who "kills" and "brings to life" the landlord is doing it to teach the innkeeper a lesson. In Rabbi Ruben's version, it's all about profit. The "rabbi test" story is based on a tale in which a farmer comes to a rabbi hoping to find out about the Talmud. Ruben's "cure" for Hal's pride is another example of a great story that doesn't fit Harvey's style, so I was glad to get it in here.

The Pretty Great Escape

Harvey's "stomachache cure" trick is based on a Jewish fable in which a fox outwits a lion. The original appears in Joseph Zabara's *Book of Delight*, written in Spain in about 1200 CE. The buying of multiple pieces of gefilte fish with the same coin comes from a classic comic tale in which two whisky merchants sell each other drinks from a barrel they've just purchased. Abigail's "what my father used to do" trick comes courtesy of the tales of Hershel of Ostropol, a famous Jewish trickster from nineteenth-century Ukraine. Her "horse spell" bit is inspired by a hilarious folktale in which a poor man borrows a donkey from a rich man, sells it, and ties himself up in the donkey's place.

Showdown at Elk Spring

A tale about the revered eighteenth-century scholar Rabbi Eliyahu, the Vilna Gaon, provides the logical gymnastics Harvey uses in his "you neither killed the bird nor cured it" trick. The mule bit comes from a classic story in which a rabbi tries to teach the lesson that what matters in Judaism is not abstract holiness, but deeds. When confronted to list all his possessions, Harvey turns to a very wise tale about Samuel ha'Nagid, vizier to the king of Granada in the eleventh century. Ruben's "cure" for blindness comes from a tale starring Maimonides in which rival doctors in Cairo try to show him up by granting the gift of sight, only to have Maimonides publically expose the hoax. Harvey's final "clean hands" trick comes from another Vilna Gaon story.

SUGGESTIONS FOR FURTHER READING

Ausubel, Nathan, ed. *A Treasury of Jewish Folklore*. New York: Crown, 1989.

Cohen, Abraham. *Everyman's Talmud: The Major Teachings of the Rabbinic Sages*. Miami, FL: BN, 2009.

*Eisner, Will. *The Plot: The Secret Story of the Protocols of the Elders of Zion*. New York: W. W. Norton, 2006.

Elkins, Dov Peretz. *The Wisdom of Judaism: An Introduction to the Values of the Talmud*. Woodstock, VT: Jewish Lights, 2007.

Kaplan, Aryeh, trans. *The Lost Princess & Other Kabbalistic Tales of Rebbe Nachman of Breslov*. Woodstock, VT: Jewish Lights, 2005.

————. *The Seven Beggers & Other Kabbalistic Tales of Rebbe Nachman of Breslov*. Woodstock, VT: Jewish Lights, 2005.

*Katchor, Ben. *Julius Knipl: Real Estate Photographer*. Boston: Little, Brown, 1996.

*Mack, Stan. *The Story of the Jews: A 4,000-Year Adventure—A Graphic History Book*. Woodstock, VT: Jewish Lights, 2001.

*Modan, Rutu. *Exit Wounds*. Montreal: Drawn & Quarterly, 2008.

Rochlin, Fred, and Harriet. *Pioneer Jews: A New Life in the Far West*. Boston: Mariner Books, 2000.

Schram, Peninnah. *Jewish Stories One Generation Tells Another*. Lanham, MD: Jason Aronson, 1996.

Schwartz, Howard. *Leaves from the Garden of Eden: One Hundred Classic Jewish Tales*. New York: Oxford University Press, 2009.

*Sfar, Joann. *The Rabbi's Cat*. New York: Pantheon Books, 2007.

Sheinkin, David. *Path of the Kabbalah*. New York: Paragon House, 1986.

*Sheinkin, Steve. *The Adventures of Rabbi Harvey: A Graphic Novel of Jewish Wisdom and Wit in the Wild West*. Woodstock, VT: Jewish Lights, 2006.

————. *Rabbi Harvey Rides Again: A Graphic Novel of Jewish Folktales Let Loose in the Wild West*. Woodstock, VT: Jewish Lights, 2008.

*Spiegelman, Art. *Maus: A Survivors Tale: My Father Bleeds History/Here My Troubles Began*. New York: Pantheon, 1992.

*Sturm, James. *The Golem's Mighty Swing*. Montreal: Drawn & Quarterly, 2003.

*Waldman, JT. *Megillat Ester*. Philadelphia: Jewish Publication Society, 2006.

Wiesel, Elie. *Souls on Fire: Portraits and Legends of Hasidic Masters*. New York: Simon & Schuster, 1982.

* graphic novels/comics